Ghost
Sister

Ghost Sister

Lynne Markham

EGMONT

First published in Great Britain 2003
by Egmont Books Limited
239 Kensington High Street,
London W8 6SA

Text copyright © 2003 Lynne Markham
Illustration and cover design copyright © 2003 Angelo Rinaldi

The moral rights of the author and the illustrator have been asserted

ISBN 1 4052 0386 2

10 9 8 7 6 5 4 3 2 1

A CIP catalogue record for this title
is available from the British Library

Typeset by Dorchester Typesetting Group Ltd
Printed and bound in Great Britain
by Cox & Wyman Ltd, Reading, Berkshire

Contents

Henry
b. 1880

Lottie
b. 1885

Grandma Mary (Lizzie's great grandma)
b. 1905

Great Aunt Sarah
b. 1915

Elizabeth (Lizzie's grandma)
b. 1935

Helen (Lizzie's mum)
b. 1965

Lizzie
b. 1993

Daniel
b. 1991

1

Kittiwakes are the souls of long-lost children

Lizzie often pretended things. Before she moved to the seaside with her mum and dad and brother Daniel, she had sometimes imagined that they lived in a house made out of shells where you could hear the sea shush and echo through them. In the pretend house it was always sunny and the sea was gentle, like a friend you could play with.

But the real house was squat and white. In the distance you could hear the sea surging and mostly it sounded angry.

'Why did we have to come and live here?'

'Because my Great Aunt Sarah left the house to us. And it belonged to her mother and father before that. We belong here. Your dad and I can work from home. We'll be really happy here, you wait and see.'

Lizzie had already waited for two whole weeks to be happy.

'I'm fed up with playing on my own.'

'Why don't you play with Daniel?' Mum asked.

Daniel was three years older than Lizzie and he'd already managed to make lots of friends. He whizzed straight out when breakfast was finished and she didn't see him again until dinner.

'Because, that's why,' said Lizzie crossly, and her mum gave her a vague, kind smile. 'Cheer up, darling. You'll make friends when the holiday's over. There'll be lots of children when you start your new school.'

But school was still four weeks away and Lizzie missed the chats she used to have with Daniel. It felt as if he had grown up suddenly and left Lizzie behind. She missed her mum and dad as well. They didn't seem to have much time for her in their new home.

Lizzie wandered outside and stood on the beach, but all she could see was white sky and sea, and white birds soaring and riding the waves. And this sea wasn't her friend, Lizzie thought, it would sweep her

right away if it could. It was like a hungry, open hand waiting until it could pull her in.

Maybe Great Aunt Sarah had felt that too? Lizzie thought of the letter she had written to them a little while before she died.

I hope you'll be happy in my little house. I've been keeping it for you these last long years. I wasn't the right person for it, you know. But you, my dear, and your fine son, Daniel, are just what we've been waiting for. One word of warning, though: take care of Lizzie. The sea can be a lonely place . . .

'Funny old stick,' Dad had said. 'Whatever did she mean by that?'

'Nothing much. She was as mad as a hatter. That's why we never came to stay.'

Perhaps she was lonely like I am, thought Lizzie. Perhaps *her* brother had grown up all at once and she had somehow got left behind.

Lizzie scowled at the sea and stamped down the beach to a ring of rocks filled with shivering water. She lay on her stomach and leaned her head over.

Under the water there was soft white sand and tiny pieces of broken shell. She stirred the water with her hand and the sand flew up in a small white cloud just as if it was starting to snow.

At the same time a kittiwake screamed overhead and Lizzie remembered something her mother had said: *Kittiwakes are the souls of long-lost children* . . . She had put a hand over her mouth afterwards as if the words had slipped out by accident. But the kittiwake sounded wild and lonely, exactly like a child crying.

As the pool settled, the sun came out. Reflected in the water Lizzie could see

puffs of cloud like ships sailing across the sudden-blue sky. The clouds curled and floated into a shape, a shape that looked like a pale, round face with long fair hair and eyes like two very deep black pools. For a moment Lizzie thought it was *her* pale face, but when she moved, the face stayed perfectly still. It did not smile or blink when she did. When she waved a hand in front of her face, she could not see it in the clear pool.

Suddenly Lizzie felt very cold.

She sat up and looked back over her shoulder, but there was nobody else in sight on the beach.

Lizzie looked into the water again just as a gentle breeze got up, and the shape seemed to ripple and disappear. She saw her own round face looking back.

Very slowly she got to her feet. She could almost hear Sarah speaking out loud: . . . *take care of Lizzie . . . the sea can be a lonely place . . .*

2
Ghost girl

When Lizzie got home the house was
quiet. Her dad was hunched over his
computer and Mum was busy making
her pots. Daniel was out with a new
friend and he didn't want Lizzie tagging
along.

Lizzie went to the shed at the end of the
garden where her mum was working. 'Did
you ever meet your Great Aunt Sarah,

Mum? Do you know what she was really like?'

Mum stood stock-still with a pot in her hand and looked at Lizzie as if she couldn't see her, but was looking at someone else instead.

She said very slowly, 'I met her once when I was a child. She was lonely living here all by herself, but she told me she had to stay where she was: "It would be cruel to leave," were her very words, "Promise me you'll come here when I've gone." She frightened me, if you want to know, but the house is perfect for us all just now.'

Lizzie's mum bent over her work again and Lizzie wandered into the sitting-room. The room was dark. There was a photograph of Great Aunt Sarah, and paintings showing old-fashioned ships

11

hung from the thick stone walls. Sometimes, when the light was right, the sea was reflected on the wall and the ships seemed to move and toss about, pitching themselves through the ghostly waves.

One special picture seemed to draw Lizzie in. It showed a ship with a tall, black funnel with dark smoke streaming from it. A flag with tulips on flew from the back and the people on deck seemed paler than usual, hollow-eyed and very thin. Each time Lizzie looked at the picture, the room seemed to tilt about her head, and she felt a soft breath against her skin, as if something had whispered past her ear.

Lizzie put a hand up to her face and turned round sharply on her heel. But there was nobody else inside the room, just the photo of Great Aunt Sarah looking at her with fierce eyes.

Lizzie had never met her great-great-aunt, but the photograph showed a lady with wild grey hair and eyes that looked straight into hers, almost as if she knew something important, but was never going to tell.

'Come on, sunshine, time for dinner.' Mr Jennings put his head round the door and gave Lizzie a great big smile. Now that they lived on the coast, her dad smiled nearly all the time. Daniel was very happy too. Only Lizzie felt lost and unsure. The house watched her as if it was holding its breath, but what could it possibly be waiting for?

After dinner, Lizzie read her book while Daniel went outside to his bike. 'Why don't you play with your sister for once?' Mrs Jennings called loudly after him.

'She's a *girl*,' said Daniel, pulling a face. 'And anyway, I haven't got time.'

Lizzie opened her mouth to say something and then closed it again. Daniel used to have time to play with her. He had never minded before about her being a girl.

Later Lizzie went up to bed and Mum came in to say goodnight. 'Don't you worry, you'll soon settle down. The next few weeks will fly by, you'll see, and then you'll have some great new friends.' Mum pulled up the bedclothes and tucked them in tight, then she kissed Lizzie's cheek and went downstairs.

Lizzie lay in bed, but she could not sleep. She could hear the surge of the sea outside. *Boom! Whooosh!* again and again, and a single bird let out a cry.

After a while she got out of bed and pulled back the flowery curtains. The moon was lost in a fist of cloud. All Lizzie could see was the lighthouse beam blinking like a bright white eye.

Suddenly the moon sailed out. It shone a path across the sea and turned the sand to a silver stream.

'Oh!' said Lizzie. She opened the window and leaned right out, and when she did she saw something. A boy was walking across the sand. Small and thin and very pale. Closer and closer he came towards her. She could see his funny ragged trousers and the large dark cap pulled over his face.

All at once the night became still. The lighthouse had closed its single eye, even the sea had lost its roar and was frozen like

painted waves. The boy carried on up the beach until he was in front of Lizzie's window. Then he stopped and stared out of two deep eyes. And slowly he took the cap off his head. He shook his head from left to right and a shower of long fair hair tumbled out.

'You're a girl!' shouted Lizzie. 'Who are you? Wait! Please! While I talk to you.'

The girl shook her head very slowly again, and shimmering hair flew over her face. The hair became a puff of cloud, spinning in the still landscape. Then the moon disappeared and darkness came.

When Lizzie looked again, nobody was there.

3
The name in the sand

The next day Lizzie got up early. Had she imagined the girl last night, just because she needed a friend? Sometimes Lizzie pretended so hard that she believed the things she imagined were true. 'You're the Great Pretender,' her dad joked, and Mum said, 'Never mind, Lizzie. At least you know you'll never be bored.'

Now Lizzie remembered the boy who

was a girl. She was sure she hadn't imagined *that*. She saw the girl's dark pools of eyes, and although it was sunny she felt suddenly sad. The girl had looked at Lizzie as if she knew something, or was asking for something Lizzie couldn't give.

Lizzie closed the window and went downstairs. She pulled a chair up to the kitchen table and kicked her feet against the legs.

'What's the matter, Lizzie? You look glum. Look at the lovely weather outside and think what it must be like in town.' Her dad was standing at the kitchen window smiling at the smooth blue sea.

Mrs Jennings gave Lizzie a very close look and said, 'Cheer up, chicken-pie. Aren't you feeling very well?'

'Tell me some more about your Great Aunt Sarah.' The words popped right out of Lizzie's mouth before she had any time to think.

Mum crumbled a piece of toast on her plate and said, 'There's not a lot more I can tell you, Lizzie. She was my Grandma Mary's younger sister. Grandma Mary had my mother and later on my mother had *me*. It's all getting rather complicated, but my family is mostly girls. There hasn't been a boy in this house since . . .'

Mum stopped all at once and looked down at her plate. Then she glanced across at Mr Jennings. A short, sharp look at the end of a frown. Lizzie had an idea of sadness again, as if it had passed like a memory down the years.

That day the sun was warm on her head and Lizzie pretended that the sea was her friend. Daniel had refused to play with her. 'You're a stare-baby, that's what you are. Anyway, I can't play today. Got to meet someone and I'm late. See you later, stare-baby!'

She chased the little waves on the beach and ran away when they caught her up. She jumped up and down and made a big splash and then caught the splashes in both hands.

After a while she lay down in the sun. High up a kittiwake circled round. *Aak! Aak! Aak!* it called and it cast a sudden swift black shadow over the place where Lizzie lay. When the bird flew above her, Lizzie felt a breeze ripple like a sigh against her face. She thought she heard

something close to her, a soft footstep in the slipping sand, creeping up behind her head.

Opening her eyes, she saw nothing there. The kittiwake had flown off out to sea and a small cloud danced in the pale blue sky. Lizzie sat up carefully and looked about. It was then she saw something drawn in the sand — tall thin letters with loopy tails. They spelt out 'Lottie', and wavered slightly as if the writer was shaky or very weak.

Lizzie stared at the letters. Who was Lottie? Was she the boy who was a girl? How had she managed to write in the sand and disappear without being seen?

As Lizzie looked at the name she felt sad again, but then a small wave crept up the shore. It stole across the wonky letters and played with them and made them run. Lizzie shouted to it at the top of her voice, 'Stop it! Stop it! Don't do that!' But the wave rushed and tumbled and swished up the sand. Then it gathered itself into a lazy frill, and when it drew back, the name had gone.

4
Sailing

'Mum, I'm trying to make a model ship – have you got any glue?'

'Can Lizzie help you?'

'No way! She'd get all the wrong bits stuck together – and besides, it's something *I* want to do.'

Mrs Jennings gave a great big sigh. 'It's on my bench where it always is. Hang on, I'd best go with you, Daniel. I don't want you getting all stuck up.'

Lizzie sat still. She felt hurt by what Daniel had said because they always used to help each other. Why did he have to be so mean now? Tears stung at the back of her eyes and Lizzie stared at the painting with the ship on it. While she watched, the picture grew dark. She could hear a rumble like a fierce storm, but sharper and louder even than that. *BANG! CRACK!* The ship seemed to lurch. The steam from the funnel got darker and darker and the thin pale faces of the people on deck dimmed into shadows and disappeared.

Lizzie drew back quickly and put a hand to her mouth. She felt frightened suddenly, and terribly cold. Her head hurt and began to feel heavy, as if a great weight was pressing it down.

'Well!' Mrs Jennings marched back in
the room. She drew the curtains to shut
out the night and then flicked a switch to
put on the lamp. Immediately, the picture
adjusted itself until it looked the way it
had before. She could see the flag and the
pale people, and the stream of smoke
rising out of the funnel. 'Our Daniel's
really good at sums. He's sorting out

measurements for his ship. I don't know where he gets it from.'

'From me, I expect!' Mr Jennings came in. 'I'm the mathematical genius here, and you're the one who's good with her hands!'

Her parents laughed and rubbed Lizzie's hair. 'And Lizzie's the one with the big ideas! What have you been up to today, Lizzie?'

'Nothing much.' Lizzie tried to smile. She looked at the carpet with its pattern of flowers and thought of asking her mum about Lottie. But what if Dad laughed or it made Mum sad?

Then suddenly she said out loud, 'Lottie's a girl's name, isn't it?' and closed her mouth up quickly again. It was as if someone had asked the question for her and taken her completely by surprise.

'What?' Mum stared at Lizzie with a puzzled frown and Dad's face froze into a smile.

'Lottie's a girl's name. Did she live here?'

'Why do you ask, chick?'

'I thought I saw it written down, but I might not have. I just wondered though, did she live here?'

'She lived here a very long time ago. It's strange you should have mentioned her name. I wonder where you saw it, Lizzie? I don't think it's anywhere in the house.'

'Can't remember,' Lizzie said. 'I might have just imagined it. It doesn't matter. I don't care.'

'Well,' Mum hesitated, and then spoke very slowly, 'Lottie lived here with her brother Henry, many, many years ago.

She would have been Great Aunt Sarah's aunt, but . . . oh, well, never mind. All of that's just history now. Will you tell me if you see her name again? Or if anything happens to make you upset?'

Lizzie shrugged her shoulders and didn't reply and her mother looked worried for a while. Then Daniel stamped into the room.

'That glue's run out, Mum – have you got any more?'

Mum pulled a face and went to the door. 'Come on, Daniel, we'll go and look.'

That night Lizzie dreamed of a ship that creaked and groaned. She could smell tar and oil and wood and coal, and hear the *dick-dick-dick* of an engine slowly ploughing through invisible waves. Then suddenly she heard the sea, not surging like it usually did, but thundering loudly, and louder still, until it crashed down with a mighty *RO-OAR*!

Lizzie sat up in bed. She was wide awake. The room was very quiet and still, but the sea still surged inside her head. She got out of bed and looked outside. The fair-haired girl was not on the beach, but Lizzie thought she saw a lone white bird fly across the crystal moon and vanish into the navy blue sky.

5
The Black Tulip

For the next few days the sun shone brightly. It turned the sea into glass again and made galloping horses of the foam-capped waves. Once Lizzie saw a snow-white seal looking at her with mournful eyes and the seal made her think of the girl.

Lottie. Lizzie said the name inside her head, and sometimes she shouted it out to the waves: Lottie! Lottie! Lottie!

Now that she knew Lottie was family, even from so many years ago, Lizzie didn't feel quite so all alone. She could sense Lottie with her on the beach. They ran and splashed in the sea together and drew patterns in the flat, wet sand. Sometimes Lizzie almost saw her. She turned round quickly with the sun in her eyes and she saw a sudden wisp of white vanish as soon as it appeared. Then the kittiwake called again *Aak*! *Aak*! and circled wildly overhead.

Lizzie told Lottie things she didn't tell her mum. She told her how much she missed Daniel. 'He used to play with me all the time. But now he's too busy with his model ship. He says I'm too young to play with him now, but I reckon that

Daniel's just too old.' She told how she missed the old house. 'It had a garden that was always green, and trees that pointed to the sky. The trees in our garden here are covered all over with wind-blown sand and they hunch themselves up like little old men.'

Usually Lottie didn't reply, but sometimes Lizzie heard a tune in her head that she hadn't ever heard before. It sounded sweet and tinkly, like small shells ringing gently together, and Lizzie began to hum it out loud.

'You're looking better, chick,' Mrs Jennings said. 'What's that lovely tune you're humming? Is it one you learnt at your old school?'

'Don't know.'

Lizzie wanted to discover some more

about Lottie, but she was scared that talking about her might frighten her off.

One day Lizzie woke up to a strange, white world. When she looked out of the window the lighthouse had vanished and the sea was just a ghostly noise hissing against an invisible shore.

'It's a sea fret,' Dad told her at breakfast. 'It's the ghosts and beasties having a ball.'

'Don't say such things.' Mrs Jennings looked cross. 'It's just water vapour, that's all.'

All that day the mist swirled round. It soaked up the sound of birds calling and blotted out the garden and the beach. Lizzie and Daniel had to stay indoors. 'I'm going to carry on making my ship and then I'll sail her along the coast.'

'Let me help.' Lizzie followed Daniel up to his room. Daniel's was the narrowest room in the house and his window was like a round porthole.

'You can if you promise to do what I say.'

Lizzie clasped her hands together tight.

At last Daniel was letting her help! Now he would remember how useful she was!

Daniel opened his cupboard, got out the ship and laid it down on top of his desk. It had a tall, black funnel and a black-painted hulk. A flag was waiting to be glued on. Lizzie touched the ship and then drew back. It reminded her of something she had seen before.

'This is the ship that's in the sitting-room!' Lizzie picked up the flag and peered at it.

'Eh? What? No, it's not. It's one I made up for myself.'

'But,' said Lizzie, and then stopped all at once. She stared at the ship lying on the desk and while she looked, her head felt strange. The tinkling tune that she liked so much changed abruptly to a cracking *ROAR*!

'STOP IT!' said Lizzie. She put her hands up over her ears.

'What's up now?' Daniel looked fed up, 'if you don't want to help me, you don't have to.'

In Lizzie's head the noise died down.

'What are you going to call her?' she asked.

'The *Black Tulip*. That's the name of a book I just read.' Daniel shrugged his shoulders. 'So are you going to help or not? If not, you can scarper so I've got more room. It's just at the really tricky bit now.'

Lizzie wanted to look at the picture again. Was the ship really the same as the one Daniel had made?

'I've changed my mind,' she said with

regret, 'I think I'll do something else instead.'

'Suit yourself.' Daniel picked the ship up off the desk and began tunelessly whistling to himself.

Lizzie went downstairs to the sitting-room. She pulled up a chair and stood on it and then gazed at the picture on the wall. She saw the tulips on the flag and the tiny people against the rail. Then she peered more closely at the bow. In very faint letters there was a name.

The *Black Tulip*.

6
Shipwreck

That night Lizzie went to bed early. She thought of the model ship and the painting. How could Daniel make the same ship with the strange name and the strange tulip flag, without ever knowing that he had? When she closed her eyes, Lizzie saw the *Black Tulip* chugging in and out of the mist. But I'm not asleep, she thought, surprised.

She opened her eyes and the ship was still there, moving across the bedroom wall. Pale figures moved to and fro on the deck, but the picture was like a silent film.

Then all at once Lizzie saw something. A flash of orange lit the sky and inside her head there was a deafening *BOOM*! Voices came at her out of the dark. There were strange cries and yells and a splintering noise, and then a huge great roaring *CRACK*! Lizzie closed her eyes as the sea swelled up and the flash of orange flamed higher and higher.

BOOM! went the foghorn outside in the mist. Lizzie put her hands up over her ears, but the noises came again. *BOOM*! and *CRACK*! Voices yelled behind her hands and a yellow flame licked behind her eyes. Lizzie smelt something like wood being burned. There was the hiss and spit of fire and sea and the babble of voices rising and falling, and then a sudden, eerie quiet.

Slowly she took her hands from her ears and looked at the wall where the ship had been. Nothing was there except the whitewashed stone gleaming faintly in the milky light.

Lizzie let out her breath in a long, low *whooosh*! and at the same time heard a tinkling sound, like tiny shells ringing in her ears. The shells swelled into the tune that Lizzie heard in her head and sometimes found herself humming out loud.

Then the mist outside began to swirl again, and slowly Lizzie got out of bed. She looked out of the window and the mist made the shape of a girl who was slender with long fair hair.

'Lottie!' Lizzie said softly, 'It's you, isn't it? How can I help? What do you want? I wish you could be happy again.'

Lottie swayed in the mist. She looked sadder and sadder, but she did not speak. Instead, the black pools of her eyes grew deeper and seemed to spread and spread like a puddle of sadness until at last she disappeared.

In the morning the light was clear and bright. The sun shone down from a hard, blue sky and the lighthouse stood firm on its huge, grey rock.

Lizzie went downstairs to the sitting-room. She stared at the picture on the wall, but it looked the same as it always did.

Over breakfast, she thought about telling Mum what she'd seen, before the other two came down. But supposing Mum thought she was pretending again? She would feel as if she had let Lottie down.

'Listen, darling,' Mrs Jennings put a hand suddenly on Lizzie's shoulder, 'you can tell me anything, you know. And maybe I can make it better? Or maybe I should talk to *you*?'

Before Lizzie could answer, Mr Jennings came in. 'Hello, Lizzie-dripping. How's my girl? Is Your Gorgeousness happy and well today?'

'I'm fine,' said Lizzie. She gave him a smile and Mum turned back to the table and poured out the tea.

'I'm off now.' Daniel came in fast and went out again.

Mum shouted at the back of his head, 'We'll expect you for lunch, Daniel, remember! And that means one o'clock, not two!'

Lizzie stayed quiet when Daniel went out. She had nearly told Mum all about Lottie, but the chance had slipped away. Dad didn't believe in ghosts – he would have laughed at Lizzie and made one of his jokes. She couldn't even tell Daniel now, because he would just call her a stare-baby.

Later Lizzie got up to go and Mum gave her a hug when she went out the door. 'I'll talk to you later, Lizzie, OK? There's an order I've to get off now. Take care, sweetheart, and don't go far.'

Outside the sea looked flat and still. There was no breeze and no clouds over the sun. Lizzie thought it was almost as if the sea and the sky were waiting to see what she would do.

'There's this kid whose dad's got a boat of his own, and he says I can sail with them next time they go – I can, Dad, can't I? It'll be OK. We'll just go further up the coast.'

'Well,' said Dad slowly, 'we'll have to

see. I'm not sure I want you sailing away. Let's see what your mum says when she gets back.'

It was lunchtime and Lizzie ate her sandwich while Daniel talked. But she felt fed up with what he said. She did not want him to sail away and leave her behind, while he saw new things.

Daniel turned to her. 'I've nearly finished my ship. I did all the painting on it last night. It's in the airing cupboard to dry.'

Lizzie frowned at her plate. Daniel had finished the *Black Tulip* without her help, and it felt almost as if he had finished with *her*.

After lunch Daniel went upstairs. All at once they heard a yell. Then his feet came pounding down the stairs. Daniel banged into the kitchen with an angry red face.

He shouted at Lizzie, 'You smashed my ship! It was fine last night, and now look at it! It's all in tiny broken pieces, I'll never be able to mend it again!'

'I didn't do it!' Lizzie shouted back. 'Why would I smash your stupid ship? I didn't even know it was where you said! Perhaps something fell on it in the night. Or perhaps it fell down all on its own.'

'It didn't!' yelled Daniel, 'It's deliberately smashed. It looks as if it's been wrecked at sea. There's nothing left I can use again. And if you didn't smash it, stare-baby, who did?'

7
Lottie and Henry

Lizzie sat at the kitchen table with the wreck of the *Black Tulip* in front of her. Daniel had stormed off to play with his friends. *You smashed my ship!* He only half-believed her when she said that she hadn't, and even Dad had looked perturbed.

'Were you having a pretend game and you dropped it?' he asked. Lizzie had felt hot tears begin to sting her eyes. How could she prove that it wasn't her?

Mum came home in the afternoon. 'Oh dear,' she said, 'Did you have an accident, Lizzie, chick? I expect we can mend it if we try.'

'No!' shouted Lizzie, 'it wasn't me! It was the ghost that did it! It was Lottie, right?'

As soon as the words were out of her mouth, Lizzie felt a peculiar sort of pain, the same pain she had when her little dog died.

'Lottie!' Mum stopped in her tracks and stared hard at Lizzie. 'Whatever made you say that, Lizzie, love?'

Lizzie shrugged and looked down at the table. Tears were squeezing out of her eyes although she didn't want them to.

'No need for that.' Mum crossed the room and gave Lizzie a hug that smelt of paint and turpentine. 'I believe you if you say you didn't break Daniel's ship, but I've been watching you for the last few days, and I think it's time we had that talk. Come with me for a moment, Lizzie, there's something I want to show you now.'

Mrs Jennings ushered Lizzie into the big bedroom and sat her down on an old armchair. Then she opened a drawer and took something out. 'I should have shown you this before, but I thought it might upset you too much. You've such an imagination, love. Great Aunt Sarah gave this to me. Lottie would have been her aunt and Henry was Lottie's older brother. Sarah said that this was important, but I'm not sure I believed it up until now.'

She handed Lizzie a piece of paper that was curled at the edges and yellow with age. Spidery writing ran over the page. Writing that Lizzie had seen before. 'That's Lottie's writing,' she said out loud. She smoothed the paper and began to read:

20 September, 1895

To My Dear Mother and Father,

Today I go to join dearest Henry. I will find somewhere to hide in the hold on his ship. When we reach Holland, I will see him again. I miss him so much when he's away. There's no one I can play with now, or talk to the way I do with Henry. It's a lonely feeling to be on your own. I want to see tulips and windmills too, just the way Henry described them to me.

The Black Tulip *returns in two weeks time. Please don't fret yourselves for me.*

Your affectionate daughter,
Lottie May

'Oh,' said Lizzie, very softly. She wanted to ask what had happened to Lottie, but in her heart she already knew.

Mum said, 'Henry worked on steamships, taking coal to Holland. It was hard work and it could be dangerous, many ships were lost at sea. And Henry would only have been fifteen. Poor Lottie must have worried about him. I expect she was lonely when he was gone. The two of them were very close.'

Lizzie thought how close she and Daniel had been before they had come to live by the sea. She looked down at the letter in her lap and tried to imagine Daniel going away, perhaps on a ship that was dangerous. She gave a deep sigh and Mum said gently, 'You've seen Lottie, haven't you? I guessed you had when you said her name. Sarah said Lottie might appear to you because she had seen her when she was young. She told me that this was a haunted house, but she thought that the haunting might end with us. We didn't tell you that story, Lizzie, just in case it made you scared. And besides, I'm not sure we really believed it ourselves. Your dad still doesn't. He thinks it's all just a silly tale and I shouldn't believe what Sarah said. Only then, you mentioned Lottie to me, and it made me wonder . . . you're not really scared of her, are you, Lizzie?'

'No,' said Lizzie, 'She doesn't scare me. And I don't think she meant to smash Daniel's boat. I think *she* was scared when she suddenly saw the *Black Tulip* again.'

'It's strange that Daniel should make

that ship without realising it was the one on the wall.'

Lizzie said slowly, 'Maybe he saw the ship and forgot about it, and then made one like it without knowing why. Or maybe the past is a kind of memory, living with us inside the house.'

She stopped for a moment and gazed outside. The sea looked so peaceful and unscary now, as if nothing bad could ever occur.

'What happened to Lottie in the end?'

Mum came and sat on the arm of the chair and put her chin on Lizzie's head. 'The ship she was on blew up at sea. It happened on steamships sometimes. Not a single soul was saved, but the strange thing was, Henry wasn't there. He had switched to another ship at the last minute.'

Lizzie gave a sigh, and at the same time she felt a soft breeze on her face. The letter rippled in her hands as if Lottie was telling her something else.

Mum said, 'Great Aunt Sarah was Henry's daughter. Sarah reckoned Lottie came seeking her childhood friend. She didn't appear until he was grown-up and she couldn't find the young boy she had known. But she could see Sarah who was your age now and on her own for much of the time. And, of course, Sarah could see *her.*'

'Yes,' said Lizzie, and stopped again. She wondered why she could see Lottie May. Was it because Lizzie was lonely too? Or was Lottie still hoping to find someone else?

Mum stroked Lizzie's hair. 'I don't know

why Lottie comes to you. Perhaps she thinks you might be friends. Or perhaps you remind her of someone else. Who knows? You might get used to her in the end, and be miserable if she decides to go.'

Suddenly Mum got up from the chair. 'There's a photo somewhere of Great Aunt Sarah, taken near here on the edge of the sea. Here it is. It's faded and torn, but you can see what she looked like when she was a young girl.'

In the photo was a girl with long, fair hair that floated towards the sea in the wind. She was looking straight ahead, and her eyes were deep and fierce and dark. While Lizzie looked, she thought she heard shells ringing faintly in her ears. Next to the girl stood a tall, fair man with a long moustache and a long beard.

'She's just like Lottie,' Lizzie said very softly. 'The same blonde hair and the same deep eyes.'

'They were as alike as two peas in a pod,' said Mum. 'And that's Henry. Dear Henry lived to a ripe old age, but he never forgot what happened to Lottie. He was always just a little bit sad.'

Mum took the photograph from Lizzie and carefully put it back in the drawer. 'I haven't told Daniel any of this. He hasn't seen Lottie, so I think there's no need. Maybe we'll tell him another time when he's not so busy with his new-found friends.'

Lizzie went outside. She walked very slowly beside the sea with the shells still ringing inside her head. They were playing a slow, unhappy tune, as if Lottie was trying to speak with music and tell Lizzie her tragic tale.

Overhead a kittiwake dipped and called. It swooped down low in front of Lizzie and she remembered that thing her Mum had said: *Kittiwakes are the souls of long-lost children.*

'I would help you if I could,' said Lizzie. 'But I'm afraid I don't know what I can do.'

Back came the cry *Aak! Aak!* and Lizzie sadly walked back home.

8
The photograph

Lizzie didn't see Lottie at all the next day. She didn't hear her special tune or feel her sigh against her skin. She didn't feel Lottie laughing with her when she played with the tiny waves on the shore. Had she let Lottie down without meaning to?

'You're quiet today.' Lizzie was in the kitchen drinking her milk and Dad was tweaking her hair on his way to the door.

'Lizzie's thinking,' said Mum. 'She's good at that. That's how she gets so many ideas.'

'Huh,' said Daniel, and humped away. He wasn't speaking to Lizzie yet because he still blamed her for the loss of his ship. Mum had told him that the creaky old house had upset the ship without meaning to, but Daniel had glared at her scornfully and turned his back and stamped away.

Lizzie sat on her chair and stayed very quiet. She missed Daniel teasing her and making her laugh. She had missed Lottie playing with her today. And what would happen if she made Lottie happy? Would she go away and never come back?

That afternoon Lizzie stayed at home. She remembered what Sarah had said about Lottie: *Lottie came seeking her childhood friend*. But Henry had died many years ago, so how could Lizzie help her now? Maybe there was a clue in the photograph that she had missed when she looked at it yesterday.

'Can I look at that photograph again, Mum, please?'

'Sure,' said Mum, 'Have you got one of your ideas, Lizzie? Great Aunt Sarah seems to fascinate you.'

Lizzie followed Mum up the wooden stairs and into the big bedroom at the front. She watched her open the chest of drawers and glance at the picture before she gave it to Lizzie.

'Put it back properly when you've finished,' she said. 'It's the only photograph we have of them both.'

Mum left the room and as soon as she

did Lizzie felt a sigh that wasn't her own. It swept round the room like a gentle breeze and teased at Lizzie's tangled curls. It whispered against the photograph and made it flutter in her hand.

'Lottie. It's you, isn't it?' she said. But the breeze crept out through the open window and the room suddenly became silent and still.

Lizzie stared at the photograph. She saw Sarah's face with her huge shaded eyes and the long hair flowing out in the breeze. She saw Henry's hand on Sarah's shoulder, his pale, sad smile and long, fair beard. But there was something important she could not see. Something she was certain was in the picture that might make Lottie happy again.

Lizzie stared and stared, but all she saw

were two people standing side by side,
smiling their wistful, long-ago smiles.

After a while she put the photograph
back and went downstairs to have her tea.

'Looks like Lizzie's lost something!' Dad
teased Lizzie again for being so quiet.

Daniel said, 'Huh!' and scowled at her,
and then changed his mind and said to
Lizzie, 'You can have this stone I found

today. It's got a fossil flower on it. I reckon it's a squillion-thousand years old. It was on the beach by Turney's Quay.'

He reached in his pocket and took out a stone, and gave it to Lizzie with a very kind smile.

Suddenly the sun seemed to shine more brightly. Lizzie put the stone beside her plate. 'Thank you,' she said, and smiled back.

'There now,' said Mum in a pleasant sort of voice. 'What a nice brother you have, Lizzie. If you find another stone, can I have it?'

For the rest of the evening Lizzie sat on her own. She did not play tiddlywinks with Mum or read her book or watch television. Instead she sat and thought about Lottie searching for her beloved brother, Henry, and never, ever finding him.

The moon was up when she went to bed but instead of dreaming of ships and waves and hearing the sound of ghostly voices, there was a strange sort of gap where the dreams should have been.

Lizzie opened her eyes and stared at the room. She thought she could hear the sound of sadness, like a distant echo creeping slowly into her ears.

Then the photograph flashed in front of her eyes. She saw Sarah and Henry standing together. And almost at once Lizzie saw something else. The one thing she had missed before stared out at her from the moonlit dark.

Lizzie caught her breath and lay very still. She pictured the photograph in her mind. Henry and Sarah. Sarah and Henry. Both of them looked like Lottie May. And so did someone else Lizzie knew. Someone who might make Lottie happy if only she could see him now.

Lizzie thought very hard, and then she gave a deep sigh. She wanted to help Lottie, but she was still afraid in case helping her meant she would go away. But if you liked someone, you had to let them be happy, even if you might not be happy too.

As soon as the thought came into her head, she heard the gentle sound of shells ringing like voices over the sea. The shells rang louder, then louder still. And slowly Lizzie got out of bed.

9
Brother Daniel

Lizzie went to the window and looked outside. A silver pathway gleamed through the sand, and the clouds and the sea had stopped again. While Lizzie watched, a figure appeared. Closer and closer it came to her window. The figure breathed a silver mist, and when she shook her head there was the sound of shells.

'Lottie!' said Lizzie. 'Wait for me!

There's someone I want to show you, Lottie, someone who I think you should meet.'

Lottie did not speak. She stayed very still. But her eyes began to widen and glow as if she was gazing through the moon.

Quickly Lizzie pulled on her dressing-gown. Then she crossed the landing to Daniel's room. Without even knocking she went through the door and straight up to where Daniel lay sleeping.

'Daniel! Daniel! Wake up please! It's important, Daniel, you've got to come with me!'

Daniel stretched and groaned and covered his face, but Lizzie pulled him roughly by the arm and threw the covers back on the bed.

'Wassamatter?' he asked, sleepily. 'Are you poorly? Stop it! Where's Mum and Dad?'

'Come *on*, Daniel! There's not much time. It will only take a minute or two and then you can go straight back to sleep.'

Daniel got out of bed in his pyjamas, and Lizzie took hold of his sleepy hand. She tugged him downstairs in his bare feet, and put a finger over her lips to keep quiet.

Outside the air was mild and sweet, and the sand was warm and as soft as silk, slipping gently beneath their feet.

'Over here,' said Lizzie. She pulled Daniel on to the silver path where the moon made them blink with its fierce light.

At first Lizzie thought Lottie wasn't there, but then she saw two eyes like golden lamps glowing through the still night air.

'Lottie, this is Daniel,' said Lizzie softly. 'He's just like Henry in the photograph. The same eyes. The same smile, but without the beard. Henry's gone but Daniel's here. He's the first boy born since Henry's time. Daniel's my brother, but he's just like Henry. And after Daniel there'll be another boy, even if you have to wait a while. Can you hear me, Lottie? Do you understand? You needn't be sad or lonely for long because a boy like Henry will appear some day.'

When Lizzie finished speaking she stepped off the path and left Daniel alone in the dazzling light.

'Who're you speaking to?' he asked gruffly. 'What's the matter? What are we doing? Why did you want to bring me out here?'

'Shush,' said Lizzie, 'just stay quiet. We'll both go back to bed very soon.'

'You're nuts, you are, you're bonkers, our Lizzie.' Daniel sounded cross and fed up, but he stayed where he was with a scowl on his face and his arms folded tightly across his chest.

Lizzie stayed in the shadows and held her breath. And while Daniel waited, a hand crept out. Not a hand with fingers and thumbs, but a hand made out of silver light. The hand touched Daniel's head and stroked his hair. It traced the shape of his cross face. Then it slowly, slowly withdrew again.

'You see?' said Lizzie. 'We're family. We all follow on from your Henry. Only

sometimes we have to wait for a boy.'

Daniel moved just then, and touched his cheek. 'A moth flew past me in the dark. Come on, Lizzie, I'm getting cold. If you want to talk to yourself, do it inside. I'm going back to bed right now.'

Daniel walked away towards the house and Lottie's eyes followed after him. Lizzie saw their glow turn from gold to grey, and then fade very slowly to an inky dark.

At the same time Lizzie heard the shells, tinkling against her ears again. The noise they made was a bit like laughing, and Lizzie laughed back and said out loud, 'I reckon Daniel's just like Henry! I expect you forgot how daft he could be!'

Back came the laughing bells again, just as a cloud breathed over the moon. The sea began to lap and pluck at the shore and the lighthouse eye shone over the waves.

When she looked again, Lottie had disappeared, but Lizzie thought she heard an early bird call a greeting across the sand. She waited until the sound died away, and then followed Daniel back to the house.

10
Happy at last

The next morning Lizzie felt very sleepy. When she opened her eyes the room seemed too bright, and when she closed them again, a soft mist swirled round.

'Lizzie!' Mum shouted up the stairs, 'Wake up, sleepyhead, and have something to eat.'

Lizzie got out of bed and went downstairs. She was afraid she might feel lonely today, but instead there was a strange sort of warmth, spreading like a smile inside her head.

'Hello stare-baby,' Daniel said. Lizzie waited for him to say something else, maybe to tease her about last night. But Daniel carried on eating and reading a book as if he had forgotten what had happened.

After breakfast Daniel went outside and Dad went to work in his small white room. Mum stayed at the table and looked at Lizzie. Then she leaned across and took her hand. 'Are you all right, love? You look a bit tired. Has Lottie been visiting you again?'

Lizzie waited a moment before she replied. She had a feeling that they were not on their own, that someone they could not see or hear was listening closely to what she would say.

Mum squeezed her hand and Lizzie said slowly, 'I could see Lottie because I wanted to, and I think that's the reason she could see *me*. She came looking for Henry, but she couldn't find him. She could never find the boy she knew because Henry grew up and left her behind. But Henry had children and in the end there was *you*. And you had Daniel. Do you see? Daniel's like a part of Henry passed down through the family. It's something that Lottie understands now and I think it's made her happy again.'

'But what about Daniel?' Mum asked, confused. 'Isn't it strange that she didn't see him? Especially now he's such a big boy!'

'I think,' said Lizzie, looking down at

the table, 'you have to be a little bit lonely yourself before you can be seen by a lonely ghost.'

'Oh, Lizzie, love,' Mum looked upset. She took hold of Lizzie's hand again and stroked it gently. 'I wish we didn't have to be so busy. Perhaps Dad and I could take a break and have a holiday with you soon. I'm afraid you'll be even lonelier, darling, if Lottie is happy and has drifted away.'

But inside Lizzie the warm smile grew. She could feel it spreading like a rush of bright water right to the very tips of her toes. She said softly, 'I won't be lonely because she's still here – she's family, isn't she? Like Sarah and you. So even if I don't see her again, I'll know that she's not very far away.'

'That's great,' said Mum. She squeezed Lizzie's hand and then blew her nose and got up suddenly from the table. 'There's something I think that you might like to see. Just wait a moment while I fetch it down.'

Mum went upstairs to the big bedroom and there was the sound of a drawer being opened and closed. When she came back, she had a bag in her hand. She opened the bag and took something out. 'Here,' she said. 'I did this especially for you, Lizzie. I know how much you like looking at it.'

Mum handed a photograph to Lizzie. It was the one showing Henry and Sarah together and Mum had framed it properly with small seashells.

'I thought we could put it over here, next to the picture of the *Black Tulip*. What do you think? Does it look OK? It's nice to have them back in the family again.'

Lizzie touched the picture and Sarah's face seemed to lose its fierceness and smile at her. 'It's beautiful, Mum. But could we have a picture of Daniel as well? I think Lottie would like it, it would make her laugh. I think she would have liked Daniel too.'

'Of course,' said Mum, 'and one of you. We'll have a family circle round the room to help us chase the shadows away!'

Much later on, Lizzie went upstairs. Her room was dark and cool and quiet. She looked out the window, but the moon wasn't there. The sea was crashing against the shore and the lighthouse winked its lonely eye.

Lizzie leaned her elbows on the sill. She could not see Lottie, but she knew she was there. All Lizzie need do was call to her and she would hear the special tune Lottie played, or catch a glimpse of her on the beach when the sun and the clouds and the breeze were just right.

But soon Lizzie would be starting school. She thought of the friends she might make there. None of them would be

as special as Lottie, but she wanted to meet them, just the same.

And who knew? Very strange things seemed to happen sometimes. Lizzie grew taller and older as each day passed and soon she might be as tall as Daniel.

Soon, she might even catch him up.